GRUNT!
The Primitive
Cave Boy

written and illustrated by
Timothy Bush

CROWN PUBLISHERS, INC. New York

In case you were wondering. . . This story grew out of a 1992 *New York Times* article about the discovery in France of the first-known cave paintings of penguins. The penguins in the paintings and story are not, however, the birds of the Southern Hemisphere we currently call penguins, but a similar-looking northern species to which the word "penguin" was originally applied. Better known today as the great auk (at least in English; the French still say *pingouin*), remains of these "northern penguins" have been found in Stone Age sites from Sicily to Sweden. The last populations, living on remote North Atlantic islands, were hunted to extinction in the 1840s. The other animals in this book also lived in France during the time of the penguin paintings, between ten thousand and twenty thousand years ago. Some are still there (ibex and red deer); some survive in other places (wild horses, bison, and saiga antelope); and some are extinct (woolly mammoth, woolly rhinoceros, aurochs [wild oxen], and Irish elk). Hunting by humans is thought to have been a factor in the disappearance of the last group, but this is by no means certain.

Like storytellers since the first campfires, I have selected, exaggerated, and just plain made stuff up, but some work has gone into getting the general picture right. For this reason, I chose—regretfully—to leave out the dinosaurs. From movies to Saturday morning cartoons, they're the best caveman cliché of all, but in the nonfiction history of earth, they were dead and gone some sixty million years before the earliest humans appeared.

**For Karen, Steven, and Betsy,
who try to see to it that I get out of the cave once in a while**

Published by Crown Publishers, Inc., a Random House company,
201 East 50th Street, New York, NY 10022
CROWN is a trademark of Crown Publishers, Inc.
Printed in Mexico
Library of Congress Cataloging-in-Publication Data
Bush, Timothy.
Grunt! the primitive cave boy / written and illustrated by Timothy Bush. — 1st ed.
p. cm.
Summary: Grunt, a young cave boy, can draw animals that are so realistic they come to life, but when the tribe's hunters kill the animals for food, their greed almost depletes the supply altogether.
[1. Cave dwellers—Fiction. 2. Cave paintings—Fiction. 3. Hunting—Fiction.] I. Title.
PZ7.B96545Gr 1995
[E]—dc20 94-27703

ISBN 0-517-79967-7 (trade)
      0-517-79968-5 (lib. bdg.)

10 9 8 7 6 5 4 3 2 1
First Edition

At the end of the Ice Age, in the south of France,
a primitive cave boy was hunting food.

He was possibly the worst hunter in prehistoric Europe.

"Grunt," said the local Tribal Chief (that wasn't cave talk—it was the boy's name), "you'll never bring home enough food to earn your keep. You're not a hunter . . . you're a failure."

"A *total* failure," agreed the Tribe's Hunters, and they all sniggered and mocked.

"I've disgraced you again," Grunt told his mother. "Isn't there some other way to get food?"

"These things take time," she told him. "You can't start right out with a woolly rhinoceros. How about practicing on penguins? The beach should be full of them this time of year."

At the beach, there wasn't a penguin in sight.

"It's hopeless," said Grunt. "I really am a failure . . .
a *total* failure."

Not wanting to go back and face the Hunters again, he
sat drawing penguins in the sand with his spear.

Drawing had the most extraordinary effect.

"Penguins," Grunt said. *"Food!"*

On his way back to the Tribal Caves, Grunt tried some other animals.

Woolly mammoths.

Bison.

Deer.

Rhinos, ibex, wild horses . . .

If the Tribe hunted it, Grunt drew it.

At the entrance to the Tribal Chief's cave, he added an extra-large cave bear with enormous teeth.

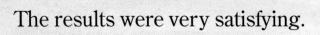

The results were very satisfying.

The Tribal Chief was none too happy about the bear, but to Grunt's surprise, the Hunters came to his defense.

"Just hold on now," they told the Chief. "This boy's brought more food in the last ten minutes than you have in the last ten years." And on the spot, they made Grunt the new Tribal Chief and told him to bring all the food he could.

That turned out to be quite a lot.

"Isn't this *enough?*" Grunt asked.
"We don't want *enough*," said the Hunters.
"We want *more*."
So Grunt gave them more.

A lot more.

"This is a bad idea," Grunt said to himself. "It's too much. This is *wrong*." He tried to tell the Hunters, but they just told him to get back to work.

Then one morning it happened. Grunt drew penguins, expecting a flock. What he got was exactly one.

"Where are the rest?" the Hunters asked.

"I think we've used them up," answered Grunt. "I told you this was a bad idea."

"Rubbish," said the Hunters.

But it was true. Grunt drew cave bears, mammoths, even the woolly rhinoceros . . . all gone. The Hunters had used them up.

"What are we going to do now?" they wailed.

The former Tribal Chief pushed to the front. "Didn't I tell you this boy was trouble?" he said. "You depend on him for food and what do you get? Failure! Total failure!"

"I tried to tell you . . ." Grunt protested, but the Hunters did not want to hear it.

Led by the newly re-elected Tribal Chief, they carried
Grunt up a mountain to throw him off.

"There's just no pleasing these people," muttered Grunt,
and begged for one more chance.

"One more," said the Tribal Chief. "Then over you go."

Grunt had never drawn fierce wild oxen before . . .

. . . so there were plenty still available.

"From now on," said Grunt, "we'll *grow* our food."

With the Ice Age ending and the oxen helping, the Tribe started the very first farm in France.

Grunt still drew on cave walls, though, and when they were found thousands of years later, his pictures of penguins made all the papers.

Grunt the Cave Boy, Total Success.